The
Friendship
Fairies
Go to Sea

The Friendship Fairies Go to Sea

LUCY KENNEDY

ILLUSTRATED BY
PHILLIP CULLEN

Gill Books

Gill Books
Hume Avenue
Park West
Dublin 12
www.gillbooks.ie

Gill Books is an imprint of M.H. Gill and Co.

Text © Lucy Kennedy 2022, 2023
Illustrations © Phillip Cullen 2022, 2023

First published in 2022. This paperback edition
published 2023.

978 07171 9742 2

Edited by Sheila Armstrong
Proofread by Victoria Woodside
Printed and bound by BZ Graf, Poland
This book is typeset in 14 on 28pt, Baskerville.

The paper used in this book comes from the wood pulp
of sustainably managed forests.

A CIP catalogue record for this book is available from
the British Library.

5 4 3 2 1

CONTENTS

To my mum and dad, thank you for
being such great parents

CHAPTER ONE
A Super-Secret
✷ Mission

'Why are they whispering?' Holly Dixon asked her sister Emme, using a tiny seashell pressed up against the living room door to hear her parents on the other side. Her tongue was sticking out in concentration.

'Holly!' said Emme in a cross voice, looking up from her homework. 'You can't keep listening in to people's conversations.' Emme was the eldest child, so she took life very seriously.

'Well, **ACTUALLY**, I want to know if it affects me, and my holiday. So, yes, I shall continue listening so that I can hear about my future, if you don't mind!' whispered Holly, going red with anger.

She was as dramatic as ever. Every year she was getting worse!

'Mum just said that she might have to work on something while we're on holiday,' explained Emme. 'She's not saying where we're going – I heard her tell Dad that it's a secret mission, and she can't even tell *him*!'

'I wonder if it's the boat thing that she

mentioned a few months ago?' wondered
Holly.

'**Boat?!**' little Jess shouted, jumping to her
feet. 'Let me get my stuff.'

She dashed out of the room. Within
seconds, she was back, wearing
flippers, a snorkel and a wrap
towel.

'I'm ready,' she panted.
Exercise was not Jess's greatest
strength, so she was always out
of breath when she ran!

'Look, let's wait and see if
they fill us in,' said Emme,
trying to keep her younger sisters grounded.
They both tended to get carried away before
hearing any facts!

That evening, their dad made them a yummy dinner of spirally-dirally green-leaf spaghetti (the fairy version of pesto). Mrs Dixon was quiet while they ate. She looked like she was trying to work something out in her head. She also had a notebook out on the table and was writing with her invisible pen. Emme tried to see what she was writing by reading it upside down, but it was just impossible.

Gemma Dixon was really amazing at her job. She worked at the Fairy Good Spy Squad company, and she adored it. She had been promoted four times in only two years, and she was now a senior spy. It was great experience for her, but it meant that she had to travel a lot. She didn't mind, as long as it didn't interfere too much with her three daughters' lives. Like all mums, being a mum was her favourite job!

'Okay,' she said suddenly, and Holly dropped her fork in fright. 'Do you remember when I mentioned that we might be going on a boat?' Mrs Dixon looked around the table at her family and smiled. 'Well, we are … sort of. We depart from a super-secret location first thing tomorrow morning. Pack after dinner, girls. That's all that I can tell you, I'm afraid. The rest, you will find out when we get there.'

'**Hooray!**' the Dixon sisters said at the same time. They gobbled down the rest of the spaghetti and ran into their room to pack immediately.

'Ta-dah,' Holly soon shouted, directing her sisters' attention to a bursting purple suitcase with bandanas, teddies and popping toys tied to it. Holly was big into turquoise, because she thought it looked 'beachy' and 'maritime'. She liked French plaits now and carried at least six skinny bobbins on each wrist at all times. She felt super cool.

Then she went outside to visit Riley, her rescue Chunga-Wunga from camp last year. Harry Barns, their next-door neighbour, was already there, brushing Riley's hair.

'Harry will mind you while we're away,'
Holly told the Chunga-Wunga, who smiled and
hooted. Riley had adjusted into their lives and
family very quickly. She had been very nervous
for the first few days, afraid to make eye contact,
but because her bond with Holly was so strong,
she trusted her. If Holly had gymnastics, Harry
would mind Riley for her — but he'd have to call
over to her, because his parents weren't animal
lovers!

'Are you sure they won't mind if Riley stays?'
Holly asked Harry.

'Leave them to me,' he said. He loved
Riley almost as much as Holly did, so he was
determined to show his parents how good the
Chunga-Wunga was. And he also wanted to
impress Holly with how good he was at looking

after Riley. Holly didn't know this, but Harry had decided that he was going to marry her when they were older. If he told her, though, she would probably box him in the nose and make vomiting noises, so he didn't dare!

As Holly waved goodbye to Riley and Harry, she felt a lump in her throat. She loved Riley so much, she would miss her terribly. She also hoped that Riley wouldn't poo on Mrs Barns's carpet and get Harry into trouble!

When Holly got back, Jess was still running around the bedroom, packing her swimming gear, a unicorn skirt, wellies and a random hoodie. She dressed herself these days, and it was always interesting!

'Let her express herself, girls,' their dad would always say if they were shocked by Jess's chosen outfit.

Emme, the ever-sensible one, rolled her clothes into little neat balls to maximise her luggage space, then added earphones and a fluffy pillow. She liked being comfortable as well as stylish.

'Right, let's sleep,' said Emme, yawning, and the others followed her routine of putting on cosy PJs, brushing their teeth and night-nighting. Even though they were excited, they all fell asleep within five minutes, dreaming of a faraway mysterious place and the sound of the sea …

CHAPTER TWO
Bon Voyage!

Yawning in the kitchen, Richie Dixon checked, double-checked and triple-checked that his family all had what they needed for their trip. It was only 7.30 a.m., and they were being collected soon to go to 'the chosen port'. It was all very secretive and private!

The taxi arrived in the form of a fly. It had been organised through the Fairy Good Spy Squad as they used the FlyBy company most days.

'Off we go!' said Mrs Dixon, talking into her
watch.

'She really is so **cool**,' thought Holly,
feeling a rush of admiration. It was times
like this when Holly was reminded just how
important her mum was.

The fly pulled up outside a small port 15 minutes later. 'Off we all get,' said Mrs Dixon, pointing to a jetty.

The girls had never been there before, and they tried to look at everything at once. The port was very pretty and clean. They could hear seagulls above them as the workers, who were all otters, prepared their nets for the day's catch.

There was also a huge navy boat with white leather chairs on the deck. There was a rumour that the yacht belonged to Sir Prize, Emme's teacher, but he had never confirmed it.

They wobbled their way down the pier, pulling their bags behind them and arguing about whose luggage was heaviest. Some of the otters slipped into the water to get away from the noisy fairies!

Waiting for them at the end of the pier was
a bright-pink submarine. 'Cooooooool,' Jess
and Holly said in unison. It was possibly the best
sight that they had ever seen. They all
walked towards the submarine, where two
octopus security guards took their luggage
from them. They had lots of arms,
but still, they nearly dropped
Holly's bags!

'Welcome aboard, Dixons,' said a man dressed in a navy-coloured sailor's uniform. He looked very smart and important, the kind of person that you can trust to know a lot about everything.

'Your cabin is 777,' the man said. 'My name is Captain Freddy Cookey, and I'll be looking after you during your stay. Anything you need, just ring the bell.'

'Sweet,' the girls thought. 'How luxurious!'

They headed for Cabin 777, where their luggage was already waiting. 'That's mad,' said Emme to her mum. 'Weren't the octopuses who had our bags behind us?'

'Ah well, love, let's just say that this isn't exactly a *normal* submarine!' Mrs Dixon leant in and whispered, 'It might even be a bit **magical**.'

'Wooooow,' said Jess in a long whisper. Her big blue eyes were fixed on her mum's. Jess loved magic, even though she was too young to have her own wand. She was really trying to develop her powers by listening in class and practising at home. A few weeks ago she had stolen Emme's wand and set fire to the toaster, so her dad had made her promise to just watch until she was old enough to have her own. Mind you, it was very funny, because she had also turned Holly's hair white! Holly had been absolutely furious with Jess, as she'd set her alarm early that Saturday to do her hair in plaits before her gymnastics class.

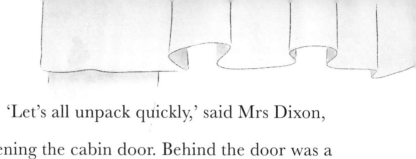

'Let's all unpack quickly,' said Mrs Dixon,

opening the cabin door. Behind the door was a

HUGE room. The far wall was made of glass,

like a fish tank, and you could see colourful sea
life outside. It had plush pink curtains at the sides
that you could close by pushing an electric button.

Emme was in her element! Since camp last year, her heart lay with the ocean and life within it. She hoped she might even see an orca, because it was her dream to ride on one. Orcas had magical powers and were believed to help fairies increase their hearing ability.

Their beds were at one side of the room, and they looked like waterbeds. Jess couldn't hold off for any longer and ran to jump up on one. *Yes!* It really was full of water!

'Wheeeeee,' she shouted, as her mum and dad looked on, laughing.

They each had multicoloured drawers under their beds, which they pulled out and filled with their clothes, shoes, swimming gear and, in Holly's case, a bag full of bobbins.

Opposite the beds was a kitchen table with six chairs – and a large cat standing beside it. The Dixons all got a fright, as he had stood there silently and completely still while they explored the room.

'Welcome,' he said in a French accent. 'I'm Julian, and I will be your **cutler** during zee mission.' He smiled at their confused faces and added, 'A cutler is a cat who is a butler by profession. I bring you now to zee boardroom,' he said, and they all followed him in nervous silence.

They followed the cutler down the corridor and into a room at the back of the submarine. As they were walking, a horn sounded and the vessel began to move – the submarine was sinking under the water!

CHAPTER THREE
The Fairy Good Spy Squad

'Welcome,' said a team of people waiting in the boardroom. They were the leaders of the Fairy Good Spy Squad, and Mrs Dixon's bosses. At the top of the table, a serious-looking man stood up. 'Senior Spy Dixon, we are delighted to see you. We think that, as the best in your field, you are perfect for this case.'

'Thank you, Jos,' Mrs Dixon said, feeling very chuffed and embarrassed with her proud family looking on – and especially with Holly clapping loudly and whistling! 'I love what I do, so thank you for giving me this opportunity. I look forward to hearing what is going on exactly. It doesn't sound good.'

'This is a **TOP-SECRET** mission, and the official story is that you are here on holiday. I will tell you more information when we get there,' said Jos. 'In the meantime, you and your family should enjoy your stay – and please let Julian know if you need anything.' The cutler did a strange little twirl.

When no one was looking, Holly and Jess silently fist-bumped. 'Let's holiday!'

Lunch was great fun. They had blobby-face pizza in the shape of an octopus. The crust was soft and full of garlic. Delish! They drank lemonade that was so fizzy and bubbly it made the girls sneeze!

Richie Dixon asked for a Sea-tail, which was on the menu as their speciality cocktail. No one knew what was in it, but it made him fall asleep lying face first in his pizza! They had to wake him up because his snoring was rocking the table.

Back in Cabin 777, Julian performed his after-lunch dance routine. It was a breakdance where he literally threw himself up against the wall and twirled around on his head. His cap was back to front, and he was wearing shades that kept slipping off. After every move, he would look up with his arms out looking for a clap like they do in the circus, so by the time he'd finished his 15-minute routine, the Dixons had very sore hands!

When the cutler finally left, the family sat
down to catch their breath. 'Ah, Gemma, finally
we're alone. Talk me through what they need
you for,' Holly asked her mum, walking over to
her with a pen and paper out.

'I'm **MUM** to you,' said Mrs Dixon in a loud whisper. Her middle daughter was so cheeky. 'I'm not sure what's going on yet, so let's enjoy our holiday until we know the plan. Who wants to come swimming?'

'We do!' said the three sisters, running around the room, frantically trying to find their swimming togs.

'Excuse me, my *petites chéries*, we are on a submarine, so you need **THESE**,' Julian said, reappearing with a funny little bow. He clicked a button and pointed at a cupboard. It opened suddenly, showing lots of shiny black wetsuits, scuba gear and equipment on a rotating wheel.

'Cooooooooool,' the girls said at the same time, making Julian smile.

They got set up in their scuba gear, which was a bit of a struggle. Putting on a wetsuit was actually very tricky and involved a lot of pulling and stretching. Wetsuits are heavy too, so after a while, their arms were getting sore! They all sat on the floor moaning and squealing until eventually the wetsuits, flippers and masks were on.

Then there was Holly's hair situation. Her
French plaits were getting in the way of her
mask. '**OUCH**, I need help, people!' she
yelled dramatically, making Mr Dixon cross.

'Holly, can you stop that, please?' he said.
'You'll frighten all the sea life away.' He tucked
in her hair for her and tried not to laugh. She
was very hard to stay angry at. She had a fun
spirit and just couldn't help being very loud!

Julian was watching them in awe. He tilted his head curiously, like cats do. He didn't realise that fairies were so noisy.

'I'll get changed now, too,' he said. He wiggled his bum, and to everyone's amazement he was immediately kitted out head to toe in scuba gear.

'You've got to be joking,' thought Holly, who was still out of breath from changing.

'How come the dancing cat gets it so easy?' She decided to keep her opinion to herself, though, to avoid trouble. No one wants to get grounded on their holiday.

'I didn't think that cats liked water,' Mr Dixon whispered to Emme quietly.

She nodded, looking confused. 'Maybe cutlers do?'

They flipped and flopped through the submarine until they reached a large wheel attached to a metal door. Julian instructed, 'We will use hand signals under zee water, because of course we cannot speak!' He sounded muffled as he had his mask on already. 'Now, get ready, everybody …'

The Dixon family helped each other get prepared, using lots of pointing and thumbs-up signals. Once they had all their gear on, Julian nodded. 'Here we go,' he said, putting in his snorkel and turning the big steel wheel …

Nothing could have prepared them for what was behind the door.

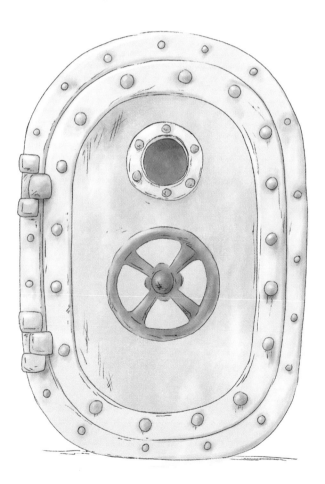

CHAPTER FOUR
Under The Sea

Through the heavy door, there was a long glass-tube walkway. It was still daytime, so the glass had daylight pouring in from the surface of the sea above them. Beautiful multicoloured fish were swimming over and around them as they slowly walked through the tube. It was breathtaking.

There were families of yellow turtles holding flippers as they swam, and mermaids waving to each other as they glided elegantly through the clear water with their beautiful long hair flowing out behind them.

'Hair envy,' thought Emme, who was currently trying to grow her hair and was secretly measuring it every day with a ruler. 'Look, Dad!' she shouted. A pod of orcas and their babies swam by, gently calling to each other.

'Unbelievable,' whispered Mr Dixon. 'Just unbelievable. What a real treat, Gemma.' He took his wife's hand, and she smiled. Mrs Dixon was very lucky. Because of her job, she had opportunities to see many amazing parts of the world, but the best part was sharing new experiences with her little family.

When they got to the end of the walkway, Julian bowed and gently encouraged them

towards a spinning rainbow-coloured circle labelled the **swisher**. This would make sure they didn't accidentally bring anything toxic into the ocean, Julian explained. Emme nodded seriously at this.

The swisher looked like a car wash, with long, soft rubbery ropes that swished around gently. Mr Dixon walked through it first, followed by the girls, Mrs Dixon and then Julian. It only took seconds, and then they were free, floating just above the ocean bed. The water felt warm and safe. It was so clear that you could see each grain of sand. All gave a thumbs up, and Julian indicated that they should follow him. He used his tail to point them in the right direction!

Through the ocean they swam, all doing lots of frantic pointing. There were stingrays, lobsters and crabs all moving around quietly, unaware of the excited swimmers above them. They were in their own peaceful world. Jess waved at everyone, because she truly believed that a smile and a wave could make anyone's day, even if they were a tiny shrimp.

After swimming for another few minutes
in awe, they could see what looked like a small
house resting on the seabed. Holly tried to wipe
her mask, thinking she was seeing things. But
when she finished wiping, the small house was
still sitting there! It looked like there was a large
bubble surrounding it.

Julian guided them over and knocked on the door twice, in a unique rhythm that sounded like a code. TAP-tap-TAP-tap-TAP.

'Come on in,' said a voice as the door was flung open. The Dixons swam in behind Julian and, as they passed through the bubble, they landed straight on the floor. They had only been swimming a foot off the ground, but still got a surprise when they dropped suddenly!

It was completely dry inside, just like a normal house. Even their scuba clothes were completely dry. Holly ran to the window and looked outside. Yes, they were definitely still at the bottom of the sea, because she could see mermaids gossiping outside as they floated by.

'You're very welcome,' said a tiny little man. He was so tiny that even Jess had to look

very hard. He had crazy blond, curly hair and was wearing a red T-shirt and a matching hat. 'What'll you have?' he asked in a thick Irish accent, walking behind a bar.

'Six *chocolatté* specials, please, Boris,' Julian said, winking at Emme.

'Right so. Take a seat,' said the voice from somewhere behind the bar, 'but don't take the sharks' corner, there's a party there today.'

They found a peach-coloured table shaped like a shell and sat down. Within seconds, six chocolatey, messy, overspilling, warm, gooey sundaes were placed on the table.

'Oooh, my favourite,' said Julian, twisting his tail in excitement. He took a few gulps, and his sundae was gone. He began to lick the cream off his whiskers.

As they all sipped and slurped in slightly shocked silence, they could hear loud noises coming from another room. Those sharks certainly knew how to party! Holly couldn't resist. Pretending to go to the bathroom, she crept around the back and opened the big door. Inside there were six sharks playing chess. They all looked up as the door creaked and seemed surprised to see a small figure standing at the door.

'Boris, have you brought us a delicious seal for **lunch**?' asked a shark with a grin. Her teeth were as big as Holly's head.

'Oh, I'm not lunch,' stammered Holly, realising that her shiny black wetsuit made her look a bit like a seal. 'I'm a fairy and actually … I'm just here to eat sundaes. Bye now!' And with that, she legged it back to her table, where her family were finishing up. 'Time to go,' she said,

trying to act calm.

'Bye-bye now!' A tiny hand waved from behind the bar.

They left in silence, as they could see that the mermaids outside were having an argument. The Dixons swam past quietly, but they couldn't help eavesdropping.

'You **LOST** my hair straightener?' shouted the blond mermaid at the red-haired one.

'Macie, I'll find it, I promise …' said the red-haired mermaid, trying to defend herself.

'Look at the **STATE** of me now, and I'm going out later, on a first date!' Macie wailed, holding out her perfectly coiffed yellow hair like she was in an ad for shampoo.

Emme looked back at the mermaids. They had no idea how truly and naturally beautiful they all were, straight hair or not. 'Why do people worry so much about how they look?' she thought as she swam quietly, deciding not to worry any more about the length of her hair. If more people concentrated on being beautiful on the inside instead, wouldn't the world be a much better place? She always judged a person by their heart – that was the fairy way.

The Dixons and Julian swam back in a row so that they could keep an eye on each other. After a few minutes, they could see the submarine. They entered one by one through the swisher and walked up through the glass tube.

'Julian, thank you so much for a great day,' said Mrs Dixon, taking off her mask. Her face felt quite tight from the salty seawater, so she was looking forward to having a nice hot shower.

'My pleasure,' said Julian. 'Get showered and have a good night's sleep. Zer are sandwiches in your cabin if you would like a bite before bed.'

So that's exactly what they did. As the girls munched happily on peanut butter and jam sandwiches, Mrs Dixon found a note under their door.

PLEASE MEET THE TEAM AT 0800 IN THE BOARDROOM.

'Here we go,' she thought, watching her daughters fall asleep.

CHAPTER FIVE
Have You Seen This Toy?

'Up and out of bed early' was Mrs Dixon's motto, so she snuck out while her family were still snoozing and arrived at the boardroom door.

'Come in,' said a voice behind the door, so in she walked.

'Okay, what's the situation?' she blurted out, dying to know what her mission would be.

'Good morning, Senior Spy Dixon,' Jos said.

He was sitting at the top of the table wearing a

hat and looking very official. He was there with

some other serious-looking fairies and a mookie

that Mrs Dixon recognised from Sir Prize's

castle. It had a round face shaped like a cookie,

with a wiggly nose and ears like a mouse.

'Now,' Jos said, very seriously, lacing his fingers together. 'There is an island near here called **Inis Bréagán**. It is a place for toys to retire to when children outgrow them or just don't want them any more. Teddies, dolls, superheroes and tin soldiers all go there. These toys were very loved, so we want them all to retire in a happy place, all together and safe.'

Mrs Dixon nodded. She was aware of this special island because she had sent her own toys there when she had outgrown them. The island and the toy home had been around for years and years. The staff who worked there were all toy specialists, trained to mind, repair and play with the toys.

'But there is a problem,' said Jos. 'In recent weeks, masked people have been spotted going on to the island in the dead of night and **STEALING** the toys.'

Mrs Dixon gasped. Being an island, Inis Bréagán had always been very safe, with a lighthouse right beside it that beamed light throughout the night. Who could be so sly and mean to do this?

'Then,' Jos continued, 'they sell the toys on the internet, illegally! The Spy Squad has been tracking the thieves' movements and it's now time to take action.'

There was silence. All eyes turned to Mrs Dixon, whose mind was racing. The island was large, and there would be a lot of ground to cover. 'Can I bring my older girls with me?' she asked.

The serious-looking fairies at the top of the table all huddled together to whisper. Jos stood up. 'If you feel that they can contribute, then yes. We will send Julian with you, too. He's a karate expert,' added Jos.

'Okay. Got it,' said Mrs Dixon. 'I'll brief the girls now and come up with a plan.'

'Thank you, Senior Spy Dixon,' sighed Jos, looking sad. He took this particular mission very personally, because one of his oldest, most beloved teddies, Sam, had been stolen and sold online. His heart felt sore thinking about it.

'Also,' he added shyly, 'if you find this teddy,' he held up a photo of a little boy hugging a dark-brown teddy bear, 'please bring him home to me. I should never have given him up. I wasn't ready.'

Mrs Dixon swallowed and nodded, taking the photo from him. She would do her best to help him.

She left the meeting room, her mind racing as she headed back to Cabin 777. Down the winding corridors of the submarine she walked, listening to the comforting humming sound of the engine.

As she opened the cabin door, she saw Julian sitting on a chair, getting his short hair brushed by Jess! He didn't look like he was enjoying the experience, but he was too polite to argue.

Mrs Dixon started pacing up and down as she briefed her team. No one dared to even burp in case it distracted her. She was in the zone.

'Girls,' she began. 'We are now lying near an island called Inis Bréagán. This island is very special because it's a place where Irish toys go to retire after children don't want to or can't play with them any more.'

Jess swallowed a lump of sadness in her throat. She didn't like the thought of anyone giving away something that they loved, even if they were ready.

'Masked thieves are getting on to the island at night. They are stealing the toys and then selling them online!' Mrs Dixon continued.

'That's a good business idea,' said Holly, out loud. She was always trying to make more cash.

'No, Holly!' said Mrs Dixon, annoyed. 'It's not good. Not good at all. These toys are tired and want to retire and relax. They love the island, where they are safe and all together. Some of them have come from the same home and have known each other for years.'

Holly nodded slowly as she began to understand. It actually was sad.

'So,' her mum continued, 'this evening when it gets dark, Julian here,' she looked over at their cutler, 'is going to somehow get us over to the island where I can catch the thieves **red-handed**!'

Julian performed his funny little bow again. Mrs Dixon nodded to him and looked back at Emme and Holly.

'Girls, I need you two as extra pairs of eyes. The island is quite big, so I might miss something important. There is a strong light when it comes from the lighthouse, but then it goes dark again. I need you to bring a torch, Holly, and, Emme, you bring your wand, just in case.'

'Dangerous …' Emme thought, getting a bit nervous and biting her lip.

'It won't be dangerous,' Mrs Dixon added, sensing her gentle eldest daughter's discomfort. 'There is a backup team briefed and ready to go on to the island once the thieves are caught in the act. They are fighting fit and ready for the challenge. But I do need you to be focused and quiet.' She looked over at Holly, who was brushing her hair and singing with a leg in the air.

'Sorry,' Holly said, embarrassed, putting down her brush and casually lowering her leg.

Mr Dixon was going to stay on the submarine in the viewing room with Jess. She was too small to go on the mission, but she didn't mind because she loved spending time with her dad. He had his own baking business and made the most delicious cakes and buns. He made their family feel safe and cosy, and he always made sure that he spent lots of quality

time with the girls. He was her hero.

Later on, Mr Dixon took the girls for dinner to the Sea Wave Café upstairs in the submarine so that Mrs Dixon could map out her evening's plan in peace.

'Wavey mash pie, please,' the girls all asked when they saw the menu.

'And for me too, please,' Mr Dixon said to the waiter, who was a black-spotted dog dressed

in a black waiter's uniform. 'A Dalmatian waiter?

A **Daiter**?' Holly whispered, and the others

laughed.

   'So, just to go through the plan again ...'

said their dad, and they ate and talked until it

was time to get ready for the mission.

CHAPTER SIX
Inis Bréagán

As the sunlight faded, inside the submarine there was a mission being prepared. Mrs Dixon and the two older girls were dressed head to toe in black, with night lights attached to black caps.

They would have to be as silent as possible on the mission, but luckily the girls had learned lots of hand signals while scuba-diving the day before.

Julian clicked his fingers five times and shook his bottom. **Whoosh!** was the noise, and a cloud of black smoke appeared. There he stood, with a bandana on his head, a tight black muscle vest, wristbands and baggy black trousers. Holly was in pain trying not to laugh out loud! Julian said nothing, just did his strange bow to the girls and took his leave.

When it was fully dark, the threesome met Julian at a special rendezvous point. 'I will help you all on to zee transport,' said Julian. He then directed them over to a lift where they waited in silence. Holly's heart was beating fast. She was so excited to be going on a real adventure with her mum and big sis.

The lift door opened and up they went. It felt like just one floor, but when the lift opened, they were at the top of the submarine, looking across the water. It glistened like a blue-black carpet in front of them.

'I will get zee boat,' Julian whispered and only then did they see a boat pop up from under the water. It was pulled by the two mermaids who had been arguing outside the café. Obviously, they had made friends again and sorted out the hair-straightener issue!

They all climbed in. Julian whistled quietly, and the boat started to move. Even though it was dark, there was a full moon and they could see the island clearly. They landed gently on the beach and stepped off on to the sand as the mermaids waited, nodding. Julian stayed behind to guard the boat. They didn't want the thieves using it to escape!

Mrs Dixon used the 'this way' signal and held her fingers to her lips to tell them not to make a sound. They crept up from the beach and could see a beautiful old building in front of them. It looked like a big white school with lots of flowers and ivy growing on it. This was the place!

The girls followed their mum around the building, keeping their eyes peeled for any movement. Mrs Dixon kept Julian updated on what was happening, whispering into her watch and saying 'over' after each sentence she spoke to him. Finally, they found the back door, which was locked.

Mrs Dixon pulled out a fairy fork and began to pick the lock while Holly and Emme kept sketch. It was so eerily quiet they could only hear their own breathing.

Finally, with a **click**, they were in.

They stood in a very large square hallway. It had a bright-red soft carpet, and there were four big doors in front of them. Each colourful door had a sign on it, reading Teddy Bears' Picnic, Dolls' House, Soldier Barracks and Action Land.

Mrs Dixon gave the girls the thumbs up to indicate that they were in the right place.

Walking slowly together, Emme and Holly approached the Teddy Bears' Picnic room. The door was slightly open, so they crept in without

making any noise. Inside was a long dormitory
with beds everywhere. There was music playing
softly around a huge picnic table.

As they snuck further into the room, Holly shone her torch, and they could see that the table was overturned, and that buns, cakes and cups were all over the floor. Worse, the little beds were all empty! The toys were all gone!

Holly gasped, and they raced back to the main hall. Mrs Dixon was there waiting for them.

'All gone,' whispered Emme to their mum. This was very serious. Who had those poor teddy bears?!

Mrs Dixon thought for a moment. 'I checked the other rooms, and the toys are still in their beds. I think the thieves will come back to steal them too. So we'll catch them in the act!'

They hid behind a huge pair of curtains that were covering a long window. Now, all that they could do was wait. And wait. And wait, holding back yawns. Patience wasn't Holly's strongest point, and Emme hadn't even been allowed to bring her headphones!

It was nearly midnight, and Holly was just thinking about lying down for a quick kip, when suddenly a door opened …

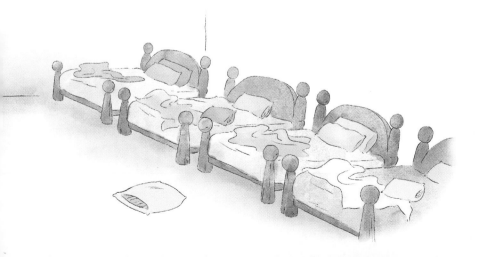

CHAPTER SEVEN
Caught Red-Handed

A door creaked slightly, and three masked figures walked out of the Action Land room pulling a large cart. On the cart was a container.

Mrs Dixon snapped into action and stepped out from behind the curtains. 'Good evening,' she said in the dark, frightening the figures. 'What is in your container?' She shone her torch at the container and then back to the masked faces.

'Ehhhh … dirty laundry, clothes and sheets,' came a muffled voice.

Mrs Dixon winked at Emme, who pointed her wand at the wall. The lights came on.

'**Laundry**, you say,' said Mrs Dixon walking towards them, sensing no danger. She was trained at negotiation, so she could sense trouble very quickly. 'I'd like to look inside, please,' she continued, talking directly to the

three masked faces. They all had long colourful
ponytails, and their masks were pink and sparkly.
'These are pretty glamorous thieves!' Emme
thought to herself.

'Well … we work here actually, in the cleaning department,' said a new voice, definitely female.

'Well,' said Mrs Dixon, 'you'll have no trouble showing me what's in the container, then, will you?' She smiled confidently.

The masked figures nodded and lifted the container lid. Sure enough, there was just laundry in it. Lots of white towels and sheets.

'Strange,' thought Emme. 'That's a lot of laundry for a toy retreat!'

Mrs Dixon felt disappointed that nothing was there, but as she turned around, she could just see Holly getting under the container. 'Oh dear,' she thought, but she decided to trust her daughter's instincts.

She kept the masked figures talking about
the weather on the island until she heard a click
and a loud squeak.

All eyes darted to the container as teddy bears, dolls and soldiers came spilling out from underneath. They had been hidden in a secret compartment under the blankets and sheets!

'Well, well, well,' said Mrs Dixon, talking into her watch. 'We've got them, over,' she said and seconds later, the front door burst open with the squad team ready to arrest the masked thieves.

'We can explain,' blurted one of the thieves. 'We were taking them back to give them to our children!'

'No, you weren't,' said Mrs Dixon. 'You've been selling them online. It's not very nice to take them away from their retirement home!'

She approached the thieves and lifted off their masks. Underneath were lady donkeys!

'Ah-ha,' said one of the squad team members. 'We've heard about this gang of lady donkeys! They call themselves **The Pink Ladonkies** and have been pulling off toy robberies around the world. Well, we've got you now!'

'Very disappointing,' thought Emme. Donkeys were usually very kind and respectful. 'I wonder why they stole those toys,' she thought, frowning.

'Wait,' Mrs Dixon said, as they were being led away. 'Do you know, or have you ever seen, this teddy bear?' She held up a picture of Sam with a younger Jos holding him.

'Yes, I remember that especially cute teddy bear,' said one of the Ladonkies, looking ashamed now. 'I will return him for you.'

They were marched away by the squad, and the Dixons turned back to the container. 'Right then, girls, before we go back to the submarine, let's take these toys back to where they belong,' said Mrs Dixon.

It took them hours, but they placed every toy and teddy bear back into their right beds. They all looked so cute tucked up in their beds. Then Emme went around and kissed them all goodnight, using her wand to add a little swish of fairy kindness over each dorm to remove any yucky thoughts.

The Spy Squad had organised new security, so as they left, they nodded at the guards at the front door. The toys would all be safe from now on.

CHAPTER EIGHT
The Pink Ladonkies

Back at base in Cabin 777, Jess and Mr Dixon were having great fun. Captain Freddy Cookey came out and joined them for a snack and chat. He told incredible stories of being at sea for the past 60 years. He really had seen it all: a giant octopus that he had made friends with called PussPusso, some very naughty pirates who were stealing precious blue pearls … you name it! Jess sat in silence and clung on to every single word. He was a brilliant storyteller.

Mr Dixon was also listening, sipping away at another Sea-tail, until of course he fell asleep again! Jess sat on his head singing loudly until he woke up.

He sat up feeling embarrassed but strangely very refreshed. 'What *is* in those Sea-tails?' he wondered.

'They are Sea Snoozers,' said Captain Cookey. 'They will give you the most solid sleep that you can ever imagine. Ten minutes of sleep, and you will look 20 years younger.'

'Great!' said Mr Dixon, laughing. He couldn't wait to see himself in the mirror later!

Just then, Emme and Holly returned with Julian. They both explained everything that had happened, talking at the exact same time and with lots of sentences starting '… and then'!

Mr Dixon felt so proud of his little family. His girls were so bright and confident, just like their mum.

Meanwhile, Mrs Dixon reported to the boardroom to tell the Spy Squad what had happened. Jos was delighted when he heard about his teddy bear, Sam. To Mrs Dixon's surprise, he even hugged her! 'Thank you so, so much,' he said, 'that makes me feel so much better.'

The Pink Ladonkies had been brought on to the submarine and were waiting in the interrogation room. This was a room surrounded by mirrors, which were actually hidden windows so that experts in body language could secretly watch them and see if they were telling lies. Jos stayed behind the windows, and Mrs Dixon stepped inside to officially question the Ladonkies.

'**Why** did you do this?' she asked the group

of ashamed donkeys. She was very tired, but

also full of adrenaline.

'W-w-w-we thought that the toys deserved to go back into loving homes,' started one of the Ladonkies. 'They are in that building day and night and … and maybe they want to go and meet new friends—'

'But,' interrupted Mrs Dixon, 'you were not only stealing them, you were also selling them online. How did you know what kind of home they were going to?! You can't see a person's face on the internet, and that's why sometimes it can be dangerous.'

The donkeys all hung their heads in shame.

'Thankfully all of the toys were chipped, so we could track them. A database has been set up, and nearly half of the toys have been returned to Inis Bréagán. As your punishment, you will all go to the island every weekend to help repair them.'

All was agreed, and the Ladonkies were taken away to sign an honesty contract, promising that they would never be dishonest again. No one had ever dared break such a contract!

'Maybe their hearts *were* in the right place,' thought Mrs Dixon, yawning. She always liked to find the good in people, but selling toys to strangers without their original owners' permission was very naughty.

She headed back to Cabin 777, where her family were dying to hear how the rest of the mission had gone. After she updated them, they all began to yawn. It was after midnight!

Richie Dixon made everyone a cup of
choccy-wokkey milk, and soon after, they all
passed out and slept soundly.

Mission complete.

CHAPTER NINE
Home Sweet Home

The last morning on the submarine, Emme woke up first. Through the glass cabin windows, she could see a pod of orcas flipping and playing in the ocean.

'Please, **please**, please, can we swim with the orcas?' she begged her parents, jumping on their bed and rudely waking them up. Mrs Dixon yawned and pressed a buzzer on the wall.

'Good morning, family,' said Julian, opening the cabin door immediately.

'Wow,' thought Mr Dixon. 'Was the cutler standing outside our door all night?!'

'Julian, do you think that it would be possible to swim with the orca family this morning?' Mrs Dixon asked.

'I shall arrange zat for you,' said Julian, doing his strange bow. 'And in zee meantime, enjoy your breakfast.'

Behind him, three trolleys filled with delicious breakfasts were wheeled in by rabbits dressed as chefs. It was the first time that the Dixons had seen these fluffy chefs!

They had brekkie and changed into their swimming costumes as the submarine began moving up towards the ocean surface. Then one by one they all squeezed into the lift. They were packed in like sardines!

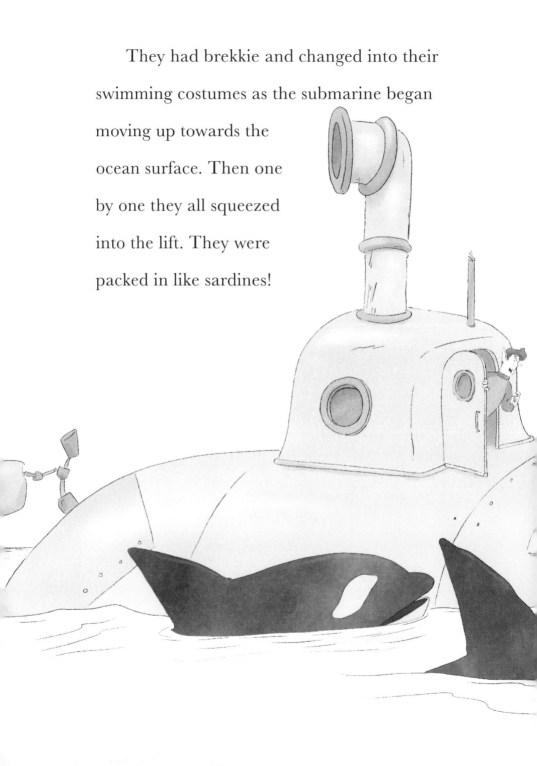

When they reached the top, they were on the surface. Emme could see that the baby orcas were waiting beside the submarine, playing sweetly. Julian made strange clicking noises to them, which they seemed to understand. Jess was very surprised to see them all nodding back!

'Go!' said Julian. 'Zey will protect you.'

The Dixon family jumped into the water, holding hands and laughing, and were immediately lifted into the air by the orcas, who flipped them gently with their tails, before landing softly back in the water. Then the orcas started nodding again.

'Zey want you to ride on zem!' shouted Julian, jumping into the water too. 'We go to Inis Bréagán again, yes?' He hopped on to an orca and clicked some more.

'Fantastic idea,' said Mrs Dixon, who wanted to see the island in the daylight. All of the toys had looked so sweet last night, and she wanted to show them to her husband and Jess.

Bumpy waves and lots of giggling later, they pulled up near the sand surrounding the island.

Julian whistled, and the baby orcas gently
rolled their guests into the shallow water, then
sped back out to sea.

'Okay, *on y va*,' he said. 'Let's go!'

It felt very strange walking up the beach and on to the path again. Last night had been so dark and scary, whereas today everything felt bright, sunny and safe. There were rolls of grass that went right down to a private beach. On the sandy beach, there were colourful deckchairs.

The newly appointed guard was standing at the door, looking very smart in a turquoise-and-white uniform of blazer, shorts and shades. His outfit suited the island life!

'Welcome,' he said as they approached the door. 'Please go on in. The toys are playing in the garden. They have completely forgotten about last night, so please don't mention it.'

'Ah,' thought Mrs Dixon, 'that is good to hear. Emme's swish of fairy magic has done the trick.'

There was music playing, and they could hear people shouting and laughing outside. The guard brought them through a new door, which led straight out to the pretty walled garden.

'Wow!' said Jess, her eyes widening. The stone walls were covered in pink blossoms, with ivy draping down the sides. And there were toys everywhere! It was so much to take in. Some were sitting on the grass in groups, relaxing, some were sunbathing in colourful sunloungers and some were being cuddled and read to by the staff. It felt so calm and friendly that Jess wanted to stay for ever!

'**Pssssst**,' said Holly, pointing to a corner.
There were The Pink Ladonkies, and they
didn't look very happy. One was covered in oil
from fixing toy cars, one was sitting at a sewing
machine and another was polishing buttons. They
were already hard at work repairing the toys!

Soon, Julian tapped his watch, and they
all sighed sadly. They waved at everyone, blew
kisses and reluctantly headed out of the garden.

'Can we not stay, Mum?' begged Jess.

'We can't,' said Mrs Dixon, looking fondly at her youngest daughter. She loved that Jess had such a caring heart. 'We have to return to the submarine now to go home. It has to go back out tonight on another mission.'

'YEESSSS!' said Holly, just hearing the words 'another mission'.

'But not with *you* this time,' Mrs Dixon continued. 'I heard Julian discussing **shark-gate** earlier on the phone, whatever that means.'

'Oops,' thought Holly, remembering the freaky sharks that she had met in the house under the sea!

After their swim, they reluctantly got back into the submarine and waved goodbye to the baby orcas. Emme was excited about testing out her hearing after spending time with them. She already felt like she could hear quieter sounds better.

'We've had such a brilliant few days,' Mrs Dixon thought, as they all packed up their belongings. Leaving, they all hugged the on-board team and thanked them for everything.

'Senior Spy Dixon,' said Jos with tears in his eyes. 'I can't thank you enough, my teddy Sam is being dropped off to me later. We couldn't have done this without you.'

'You're so welcome,' said Mrs Dixon, holding on to her little team of daughters. She was so proud of them.

'Bye, everyone,' they all shouted as they got into a FlyBy taxi back to their cosy little home.

When they got back, Holly ran straight into Harry's house to collect Riley. She was dying to see her little friend. And Harry too, of course!

'Ah, I think … I need a holiday,' said Emme,

opening their front door, and they all laughed at the same time.